Magic Ponies

A New Friend

To Silver, so exciting and an early inspiration—SB

GROSSET & DUNLAP
Published by the Penguin Group
Penguin Group (USA) Inc., 375 Hudson Street, New York, New York 10014, USA
Penguin Group (Canada), 90 Eglinton Avenue East, Suite 700, Toronto, Ontario M4P 2Y3, Canada
(a division of Pearson Penguin Canada Inc.)
Penguin Books Ltd, 80 Strand, London WC2R 0RL, England
Penguin Ireland, 25 St Stephen's Green, Dublin 2, Ireland (a division of Penguin Books Ltd)
Penguin Group (Australia), 707 Collins Street, Melbourne, Victoria 3008, Australia
(a division of Pearson Australia Group Pty Ltd)
Penguin Books India Pvt Ltd, 11 Community Centre, Panchsheel Park, New Delhi—110 017, India
Penguin Group (NZ), 67 Apollo Drive, Rosedale, Auckland 0632, New Zealand
(a division of Pearson New Zealand Ltd)
Penguin Books, Rosebank Office Park, 181 Jan Smuts Avenue, Parktown North 2193, South Africa
Penguin China, B7 Jaiming Center, 27 East Third Ring Road North,
Chaoyang District, Beijing 100020, China

Penguin Books Ltd., Registered Offices: 80 Strand, London WC2R 0RL, England

Text copyright © 2009 Sue Bentley. Illustrations copyright © 2009 Angela Swan. Cover illustration
© 2009 Andrew Farley. First printed in Great Britain in 2009 by Penguin Books Ltd. First published in
the United States in 2013 by Grosset & Dunlap, a division of Penguin Young Readers Group, 345 Hudson
Street, New York, New York 10014. GROSSET & DUNLAP is a trademark of Penguin Group (USA) Inc.
Printed in the U.S.A.

Library of Congress Cataloging-in-Publication Data is available.

ISBN 978-0-448-46205-9   10 9 8 7 6 5 4 3 2

Magic Ponies

A New Friend

SUE BENTLEY

illustrated by Angela Swan

Grosset & Dunlap
An Imprint of Penguin Group (USA) Inc.

Prologue

"Wait for me!" Comet cried, launching himself into the night sky.

Moonlight gleamed on the pony's golden wings, cream coat, and flowing golden mane and tail. His deep-violet eyes flashed as happiness flowed through him. He loved playing chase with his twin sister.

"Hurry up, lazybones! You'll never catch me!" called Destiny. She swooped teasingly close and then shot upward to hide in a fluffy cloud.

Comet noticed the rainbow dazzle of a jewel on a chain around her neck. He gasped. Destiny was wearing the Stone of Power! The stone protected the Lightning Herd they belonged to and kept them all hidden from the dark horses who would like to steal their magic. It was forbidden to take it from Rainbow Mist Island where they lived.

"Destiny! Wait! Come back!" Comet ordered.

But his twin's laughter floated toward him on the still, cold air. Comet flexed his golden wings and zoomed upward in a spurt of speed. Soaring higher and higher, he burst through the cloud and emerged into star-studded blackness.

Destiny was just ahead of him. She turned, and her ears twitched with mischief as she folded her wings and prepared to dive.

Comet called to her. "No, don't! The Stone . . ."

Ching! There was a tiny sound in the silence as the chain around Destiny's neck snapped.

"Oh no!" A chill ran through Comet as the magic stone plunged into the lake below with barely a ripple.

Destiny's eyes widened in panic.

"What have I done?" she gasped.

"We must find the stone. Follow me!" Comet urged, flying down to the water and plunging in. Destiny followed him.

It was freezing cold and pitch black in the depths of the lake. The two ponies searched for a long time, but the stone was nowhere to be seen. Comet was ready to give up, when he saw a faint glimmer on the lake's bottom. With one final effort, he dived and managed to pick up the stone.

"I have it!" But Comet broke the surface to find himself alone. Where was Destiny?

The young pony quickly flew home to Rainbow Mist Island to find his mischievous twin and tell her that all was well.

As Comet landed on the island's lush grass, an older horse with a wise expression stepped out from behind some trees.

"Blaze!" Comet dipped his head in a bow before dropping the magic stone at the leader of the Lightning Herd's feet. It lay there glowing with shifting rainbow light.

"Well done, Comet," Blaze said in a deep voice. "Your sister acted rashly, but you have saved our herd from disaster."

Comet defended his twin. "Destiny meant no harm. I'm sure she means to say sorry right away. Where is she?"

"Destiny has run away," Blaze said gravely. "It seems she thought the stone was lost forever and was afraid that she would be in terrible trouble."

"But where could she have gone?" Comet asked, puzzled.

"We do not know. You must ask for the stone's help to find her."

As Comet looked down at the stone, it began to grow larger. Rays of dazzling rainbow light spread outward, and an image formed in the center of it. Comet saw Destiny's hooves touch down in an unfamiliar forest in a world far away.

The magic pony felt a pang as he thought of his twin sister: lost, alone, and in danger. He had to find her! There was a bright flash of dazzling violet light, and a whirlwind of rainbow mist swirled around Comet. Where the magnificent winged-pony had been now stood a sturdy chestnut pony with a sandy mane and tail and glowing violet eyes.

"Go now, young friend," Blaze urged. "Use this disguise to find Destiny before she is discovered by the dark horses."

Comet's chestnut coat bloomed with violet sparks. He snorted softly as he felt his magical power building. The cloud of rainbow mist began to spin faster and faster and drew Comet in . . .

Chapter ONE

"It's so gorgeous here!" Eleanor Gale exclaimed. "I can't wait to meet Aunt Pippa's new ponies!"

She looked at Oak Cottage, which stood on the edge of a forest. Roses rambled around the front door and colorful flowers filled the front garden.

Eleanor's mom smiled. "Somehow I don't think you're going to mind spending your school vacation here while your dad and I are away."

Both Eleanor's parents were musicians in an orchestra. She'd had the chance of going on tour with them, but had instead chosen to accept the invitation to stay with her aunt.

"Spending all day riding or hanging about in boring hotel rooms? It's no contest!" Eleanor said.

Her dad smiled indulgently as he began unloading her luggage. He wasn't at all into horses and was amused by Eleanor's obsession with ponies. "Here you go." He tossed her the bag containing her riding equipment.

"Thanks!" Eleanor caught it deftly and walked through the front gate just as the cottage door opened and her aunt came out.

"Eleanor! It's great to see you!" Pippa Treacy gave her niece a hug. She was a tall, slim woman with curly brown hair. Her eyes looked very blue in her tanned face.

"Hi, Aunt Pippa!" Eleanor returned the hug. "I love your new cottage!"

"Me too. I can't believe that I've been here for six months already. You're my first overnight guest." Pippa was Eleanor's mom's older sister. She was a photographer and made her living taking pictures of wildlife.

"How's the work going for your exhibit?" Mrs. Gale asked.

"Don't ask!" Pippa sighed, tucking a strand of hair behind one ear. "I've got so much to do. I can't believe I'm ever going to be ready."

"Well, maybe Eleanor will be able to give you a hand with something," Mrs. Gale suggested. "She's pretty good with a computer."

"Um . . . yeah," Eleanor said, distracted. All she could think about was being allowed to ride her aunt's ponies soon. She was desperately going to miss her favorite pony, Patch, who she rode at riding school on the weekends, but being able to ride here every day definitely made up for it! She wondered if she would have a favorite at the end of her vacation—it would be like having her very own pony!

"I'm really sorry that we don't have time to come inside, but we're already running late," her mom said, hugging her sister. "I promise that we'll stay with you for the whole day when we come to pick up Eleanor."

"That would be great!" Pippa said, smiling. "Well—you'd better get going or you'll miss your plane. Have a good trip. And don't worry about Eleanor. We'll be fine, won't we, honey?"

Eleanor nodded at her aunt, kissed her mom and dad good-bye, and then stood

beside Pippa to wave to them as they
drove off. She suddenly felt really sad at
the thought of not seeing them for six
weeks.

As soon as her parents' car was out of
sight, Aunt Pippa took Eleanor into the
cottage and showed her to her bedroom.
It was a pretty, sunny room at the back of
the house. From the window was a view

of the neat back garden, which had a gate
that opened directly onto the forest.

Eleanor noticed that there didn't
seem to be a paddock or any barns.
She wondered where her aunt kept her
ponies.

Wow! This place is pony paradise, she
thought, looking at the pathways that
wound through the enormous trees and
clearings of purple heather and scrubby
grass. Sun shone through the trees and
glinted on a little stream off to one side.
She imagined all the wonderful rides
she'd have.

"Can we go and see your ponies
now?" Eleanor burst out, unable to
control her excitement any longer. "Are
they at a farm or stables? How many do
you have? What are their names?"

Her aunt laughed. "Slow down, Eleanor! One question at a time! I have three: Mary, Jed, and Blue. But going to see them is easier said than done. Free-ranging ponies can wander for long distances. It can take ages to track them down."

Eleanor frowned. What did her aunt mean about her ponies being free-ranging? "But I thought you owned them."

"I do, but it's not quite that straightforward," Pippa explained. "I'm what's called a commoner. That's someone who lives in a house in the forest and who has certain rights—like the right to graze ponies in the forest. My ponies are wild and pretty much take care of themselves in the summer. They have a job to do: looking after the forest."

Eleanor was fascinated. She had never
heard of a commoner before. "Are there
lots of wild ponies living in the forest and
looking after it?"

"About four thousand. They're all
owned by other commoners. We give
them hay in the winter, pay for health
checks, make sure they wear fluorescent
collars to keep them safe at night, and
so on. There are regular roundups, too,
when the herds are thinned out and some
of the ponies are sold."

"But how do you find them when
you want to ride them?" Eleanor asked
eagerly.

Aunt Pippa looked surprised. "I *don't*
ride them. None of my ponies are broken
in. I'm thinking of buying one to ride

eventually, but it's just another thing I haven't gotten around to."

"Oh, okay." Eleanor didn't know what to say. She wouldn't be able to do any riding this vacation at all! Eleanor began to miss her mom and dad even more and wondered whether she should have gone with them on tour after all.

She tried hard not to let her aunt see

how disappointed she felt. "Well, I guess it could be fun going out on a pony hunt to find Mary, Jed, and Blue," Eleanor said with forced brightness.

"They are really quite special," Aunt Pippa said, smiling. "That's why I love to photograph them. I go out looking for the ponies whenever I get the chance. Even if I can't find them there are usually others around."

Eleanor cheered up a bit at the prospect of meeting her first-ever wild pony. "I'll go and change my shoes before we go into the forest! I'll be right back!" she said eagerly.

Pippa laughed. "Whoa there, young lady! I didn't mean we could go right this minute. I'm afraid I have to head into town now to collect some prints I've had framed and organize the invitations. We can go out searching for ponies tomorrow or the day after. Why don't you come along with me for the ride? You could explore the local stores while I'm at the framer."

Eleanor didn't really feel like shopping. "I think I'll stay here and unpack, if that's okay."

"Fine by me. But are you sure you'll be all right by yourself?"

"Positive. I'm nearly ten now, Aunt Pippa. I'll sit and read in the garden when I'm finished."

Pippa beamed at her. "Goodness me! How grown up you are. Okay then, I won't be long. I'll bring us something nice back for dinner. How about pizza?"

Eleanor nodded. "Sounds good."

Her aunt went downstairs. Eleanor heard a car start up and drive off. She sank glumly onto the pretty patchwork quilt that covered her bed and allowed the disappointment to wash over her.

With no ponies to ride, it looked like this was going to be a very lonely summer. Aunt Pippa was lovely, but it was obvious she was going to be really busy getting ready for her exhibit over the next few days. Eleanor tried hard not to wish that she hadn't come. There wasn't even anyone her own age to hang out with.

She got up and put her riding boots and hat in the closet since it didn't look as if she'd have much use for them. After piling the rest of her clothes into the chest of drawers, she picked up her book and went back downstairs.

Eleanor wandered slowly outside into the garden. She went and sat on the lawn for a while, enjoying the warm smell of newly cut grass. Midafternoon sun tipped the tops of the trees with dusty gold light. A robin hopped on to a fence post, looking at Eleanor with its head to one side. It flew off as she put down her book, got up, and walked to the edge of the garden.

Resting her arms on the low garden gate, Eleanor stood staring across the forest clearing. Beyond the patches of heather and dusty-looking grass, she could see a rough path leading into a grove of birch, ash, and oak. She wondered if her aunt's ponies might be somewhere in those trees, watching her with shy, wary eyes.

Suddenly, a sparkling rainbow mist
filled the entire clearing, and Eleanor saw
rainbow droplets forming and twinkling
on her skin.

"Oh!" Eleanor squinted to try to see
through the strange mist.

As it slowly cleared, Eleanor noticed
that a pony had stepped out of the forest

and was walking slowly toward her. It had a glossy chestnut coat, a sandy mane and tail, and large, deep-violet eyes.

"Can you help me, please?" it asked in a velvety whinny.

Chapter TWO

Eleanor's jaw dropped as she stared at the pony in utter amazement. She hadn't ever seen a real wild pony before, but she was certain that ponies couldn't talk. She shook her head. She must be imagining things.

She clicked her teeth encouragingly. "Hello there. Aren't you gorgeous? I bet you've come to see if Aunt Pippa has an

apple for you. I wonder which one you are: Mary, Jed, or Blue."

The pony's ears flickered, and it lifted its head proudly. "I am neither of those. I am Comet of the Lightning Herd. I have just arrived here from Rainbow Mist Island."

"Y-you really c-can talk?" Eleanor stuttered. "How come?"

"All the magical Lightning Horses in my herd can talk. What is your name?" Comet asked.

"I–I'm Eleanor. Eleanor Gale," she found herself saying. "I'm staying here with my aunt for my summer break." She felt like pinching herself to make sure she wasn't dreaming. But Comet still stood there, looking at her calmly. She noticed again his large bright violet eyes.

Comet dipped his head in a formal bow, and his sandy mane swung forward. "I am honored to meet you, Eleanor."

"Um . . . me too." Eleanor still couldn't quite believe that this was happening, but her curiosity was starting to overtake her shock. Despite being wild, this magical pony didn't seem to be at all nervous around her. "But why are you here in the forest?" she asked.

"I am looking for my twin sister, who is lost and in hiding," Comet told her. "She is called Destiny."

"That's a lovely name. But who is she hiding from?" Eleanor asked, puzzled.

Comet's large eyes glistened with sadness. "We were playing our favorite game of cloud-racing in the night sky when Destiny accidentally lost the Lightning Herd's Stone of Power. I found the stone, but Destiny thought it was gone forever and imagined she was in a lot of trouble, so she ran away. The stone showed me that she is here, in your world. I must find her before she is discovered by the powerful dark horses who want to steal our magic."

Eleanor frowned as she tried to take this in. It all sounded so strange and unreal—like a fairy tale. "You say you and Destiny were *cloud-racing*? But how . . ."

"Please, stand back," Comet ordered, backing away.

Eleanor felt a strange warm prickling sensation flow to the tips of her fingers as violet-colored sparkles blossomed in Comet's chestnut coat, and a light rainbow mist swirled around him. The sturdy forest pony disappeared and in its place stood a handsome cream-colored pony, with a flowing golden mane and tail. Magnificent golden wings covered with gleaming feathers sprung from his shoulders.

Eleanor was speechless with wonder. She had never seen anything so beautiful in her whole life.

"Comet?" she gulped when she could
finally speak.

"Yes, it is still me, Eleanor. Do not be
afraid." Comet gave a deep musical neigh.
There was a final swirl of sparkling mist,
and Comet reappeared as the sturdy
chestnut pony.

"Wow! That's an amazing disguise!

No one would ever know that you're not an ordinary forest pony," Eleanor said.

"Destiny, too, will be in disguise. But that will not save her if the dark horses discover her," Comet said gravely. "Now I must look for her. Will you help me?"

Eleanor felt a second of doubt at the thought of the dangerous dark horses who were pursuing Comet's twin sister. But then the magic pony leaned forward and pushed his satiny nose into her hand.

Eleanor's soft heart melted as Comet huffed warm breath onto her fingers. "Of course I will!" she said. "We'll search for Destiny together."

"Thank you, Eleanor."

"I can't wait to tell Aunt Pippa about you! She'll be so—"

Comet lifted his head. "No! You must tell no one about me or what I have told you!"

Eleanor felt disappointed that she couldn't confide in her aunt. She felt sure that Aunt Pippa could be trusted.

"You must promise," Comet insisted, blinking at her with his intelligent, deep-violet eyes.

Eleanor nodded slowly. If it would help to keep Destiny safe until Comet could find her and return to Rainbow Mist Island, she was prepared to agree. "Okay. I promise. Cross my heart."

"Thank you, Eleanor."

"But where shall we start looking?" she asked. "There are thousands of ponies in the forest. If Destiny's hiding among them, it'll be almost impossible to find her."

As Comet looked thoughtful, there
was the sound of a car pulling in to the
driveway.

Eleanor exclaimed, "Aunt Pippa! She's
back. I can't come with you now. She'll
notice I'm gone. I'll have to try to sneak
out later. You'd better hide before she
sees you!"

"Very well." With a swish of his

sandy tail, the chestnut pony turned and galloped into the trees.

"Eleanor? Where are you, honey? I hope you like pepperoni on your pizza!" Aunt Pippa called from the kitchen.

"I love it! Coming!" Eleanor answered.

As she went back inside, she bit back a huge grin. It looked like her rather lonely summer had just taken a turn for the better. Never in her wildest dreams had she expected to make friends with a magic pony!

Chapter
THREE

Eleanor's heart beat fast as she peeped into the living room where Aunt Pippa was lying on the sofa, taking a short nap after dinner. All was silent, and then she heard a faint snore.

Smiling to herself, Eleanor tiptoed into the kitchen. She was already wearing her jeans and a long-sleeved top, and she sat on the back doorstep to pull on her riding boots and hat. She felt tense with excitement. Would Comet still be there? Or would he have galloped off alone to look for Destiny?

As Eleanor walked through the gate at the bottom of the back garden, the chestnut pony stepped out of the trees, and a warm orange sunset glowed behind him.

"You're still here! I'm so glad," Eleanor exclaimed.

Comet bent his neck to bump his nose very gently against her arm. "Greetings, Eleanor. Climb on to my back. We must go."

Eleanor scrambled onto the chestnut pony. She wasn't used to riding bareback, but the moment she sat astride Comet she felt perfectly at ease. His magic seemed

to spread over her, making her feel warm
and safe.

She twined her hands in Comet's
thick sandy mane as he leaped forward
and galloped into the forest. Huge oak
trees spread their branches overhead as
they followed bridleways and paths. They
came to a picnic area with a closed café
and sped past, pushing deeper into the

forest. There was no one around. Most visitors had left to go home by now.

Eleanor and Comet weaved along twisting paths and tracks. In the warm glow of the setting sun they came upon small herds of ponies, grouped together in clearings or standing under the trees. Each time, Comet paused and trotted up to them, snorting a greeting, but did not find Destiny among any of the ponies.

Comet galloped on tirelessly, his hooves skimming the ground. Eleanor crouched low on his back, feeling the breeze rush by, her hair streaming behind her. She was breathless with the thrill of riding the magic pony.

"Hold tight!" Comet told her as he surged up a hill topped by birch trees.

He paused at the top where the
ground fell away into a deep ravine and
a waterfall foamed into a river far below.
From their position on the high ground,
Eleanor could see the forest spreading out
in all directions—its hundreds of acres
of trees, divided by paths, clearings, and
roads used by tourists and visitors.

"The forest is never-ending," Eleanor
said. "How will we ever find Destiny?"

Comet had stretched his neck and was peering around with his keen eyes. "Because we are twins, we have always had a special bond. If Destiny is close, I will sense her presence. Also, if she has passed by at any time she will have left a trail."

"A trail? What will it look like?" Eleanor asked.

"There will be softly glowing hoofprints, which are invisible to most people in this world."

"Will I be able to see them?" Eleanor asked.

"Yes. If you are riding me or if I am very close to you," Comet told her. "Are you ready, Eleanor? We must keep searching."

"I'm ready!"

Comet sprang forward. He was

wonderful to ride—so smooth, fast, and exciting. Eleanor kept a close lookout but she saw no sign of any magical hoof prints, and although they met other wild ponies, none of them was Destiny.

Despite the thrill of riding Comet, Eleanor felt her eyes drooping, and she bit back a yawn. The sun was now very low in the sky. Eleanor knew that Aunt Pippa might wake at any moment.

"You are tired, Eleanor," Comet said with concern. "I will take you back now."

Back in the clearing outside her aunt's garden gate, Comet stopped and let Eleanor slide off his back.

The pony's chestnut head drooped a little. Eleanor guessed that Comet was missing his twin sister.

"We'll find Destiny," she said, gazing into his large sad eyes, which were as beautiful as amethysts. "I promise I'll do all I can to help."

"Thank you, Eleanor," Comet said gratefully. "I will see you very soon." With a flick of his tail, he whirled around and melted into the trees.

Eleanor crept into the house and went swiftly upstairs. She took off her riding boots and hat, and heard her aunt stirring. She stood at the top of the stairs just as Pippa came out into the hall.

"My goodness! I must have dozed off. I think I'm ready for bed," Pippa said, hiding a yawn behind her hand.

"Me too. Good night, Aunt Pippa. See you in the morning!" she called.

Tired, but with her thoughts still full of the thrilling forest ride, she went to her room, undressed, and crawled into bed. Moments later, she was fast asleep.

Eleanor woke to find bright yellow light flooding into her room. She threw back the patchwork quilt, her mind buzzing with all that had happened the day before.

She looked out her window toward the forest, wondering where Comet was and what he was doing. She could see no sign of him and didn't dare call out in case her aunt heard. Dressing quickly, Eleanor hurried downstairs.

Aunt Pippa was in the kitchen making breakfast. "Good morning, honey. Sleep well?" she asked.

"Yes, fine, thanks," Eleanor said, helping herself to toast and scrambled eggs. All she could think about was going into the forest to find Comet, but she needed to think of a reason for going off by herself. Aunt Pippa wasn't just going to let her wander off without knowing exactly where she was going.

Eleanor puzzled over the problem as she nibbled a corner of toast. She was

starting to think that it was all hopeless and
that yesterday might even be the only time
she would see Comet when the telephone in
the hall rang.

Aunt Pippa went to answer it and
returned looking a little flustered.

"That was the gallery. They're short-
staffed because someone is sick and wondered
if I'd mind going in and hanging my

photographs," she explained. "I think I'm going to have to go over there. I'm sorry, Eleanor. It's going to be boring for you to come with me and sit around waiting."

"Why don't I stay here? Then you won't have to worry about me," Eleanor said helpfully, trying not to sound too eager. "I want to finish my book, anyway."

Aunt Pippa looked relieved. "Well, okay. I hope I'll only be a couple of hours. Maybe we could go out and look for Mary, Jed, and Blue after lunch?"

Eleanor nodded, smiling. "I'd like that."

As soon as she'd said good-bye to her aunt, Eleanor hurried upstairs to grab her riding boots and hat and ran out the back garden gate. She stood in the clearing, her pulse quickening with excitement as she faced the trees and called Comet's name.

For a moment, nothing happened
and she almost wondered if yesterday's
thrilling ride had been a dream. But then
the chestnut pony appeared out of nowhere
and walked toward her. His sandy mane
and tail stirred in the breeze.

"Greetings, Eleanor."

"Comet!" Eleanor's heart lifted as she
looked at him, thinking how amazing it

was that he had chosen her to be his friend.
Comet was her own special secret that she
would never, ever tell anyone. "I've got
two hours to myself. We can go looking
for Destiny again!" she cried.

Comet pawed at the ground, his
deep-violet eyes flashing with eagerness.
"Thank you, Eleanor. Climb onto my
back."

Chapter FOUR

Comet set off in a different direction from the one they had taken yesterday. As they galloped between the trees, Eleanor leaned forward and entwined her hands in the pony's thick mane again. Comet moved so smoothly that she felt like a part of him and hardly even needed to grip his sides with her legs.

It suddenly occurred to Eleanor that

she shouldn't ride Comet bareback and
without a head collar in broad daylight.
They hadn't met any other riders yet,
but when they did she was sure to attract
attention.

Comet's ears twitched back as if he
felt her hesitation, and he came to a halt
beneath a large oak tree. "Is something
wrong, Eleanor?"

"It's just that in this world ponies
usually wear saddles and bridles when
they're being ridden," she told him.

Comet listened carefully as she
described the equipment in detail. When
she had finished, he nodded. "I did not
know this. No one has ever ridden me
before. I will see to it now."

Eleanor climbed down from Comet
and stood watching him curiously.

She felt a strange warm tingling sensation in her fingertips as bright violet sparks ignited in Comet's chestnut coat. His ears and tail crackled with tiny lightning bolts of magical power.

Eleanor's eyes widened. Something very strange was happening. She watched in complete astonishment as with a whooshing noise thousands of tiny glittery lights like busy worker bees sprang into the air. The sparkling crowd weaved back and forth. *Crackle! Rustle! Clink!* The lights created a full set of tack just as she'd described it.

"Wow!" Eleanor said breathlessly. Seconds later, Comet stood there fully saddled up.

"Is this right, Eleanor?" Comet asked as the sparks faded from his chestnut coat.

"It's just perfect!" Eleanor adjusted
the girth and slipped two fingers under
the strap to make sure it was firm but
not too tight around Comet's middle.
She mounted, checked her stirrup length,
picked up the reins, and they set off again.

Eleanor and Comet rode along
narrow pathways bordered by birch trees.
Gradually the trees grew thicker and

shadowed the forest floor. They rounded
some bushes and came to a clearing
where a herd of about ten wild ponies
were gathered.

"Oh look. There are some young
ones with them. Aren't they gorgeous?"
Eleanor sighed.

Comet slowed to a walking pace. He
gave a friendly nicker as he moved toward
the rather nervous-looking ponies. They
turned their heads to look at him, their

ears twitching with curiosity.

Suddenly a dog came out of nowhere and shot straight past them. Barking loudly, it ran toward the herd. One of the young wild ponies reared up, its eyes rolling in terror.

"Bad dog! Get away from them!" Eleanor shouted. She twisted around to see if an owner was visible, but there was no one in sight.

The wild ponies stamped around, blowing in alarm. The youngsters seemed ready to bolt in all directions at any moment. Eleanor was worried that they'd hurt themselves if they ran off in a blind panic.

"We'd better scare that dog off before those ponies scatter!" she cried.

Eleanor was about to squeeze Comet

gently and urge him forward when he
tossed his head nervously and backed up.
She realized that he was also scared of the
dog. Perhaps they didn't have them on
Rainbow Mist Island.

"It's okay, Comet. I'll deal with this,"
she said, quickly dismounting and running
toward the dog. But now that she was closer
to it, it seemed a lot bigger and fiercer.

"Go away! Go on!" she cried, waving
her arms.

The dog turned and looked at her, and
a growl rumbled in its throat. It started
to walk toward her. Eleanor gulped and
began to back up slowly, regretting her rash
decision to face the dog alone.

She felt another prickling sensation
in her fingertips. It was a lot softer than
last time.

She glanced at Comet and watched
as the chestnut pony opened his mouth
and huffed out a big breath, which turned
into a miniature violet fireball. It shot
toward the dog, trailing bright sparks,
and hit it harmlessly on the nose before
dissolving into a puff of smoke. *Poof!*

"Yip!" The dog gave a surprised yelp and dashed headlong for the trees with its tail between its legs.

Eleanor let out a sigh of relief. She walked back to Comet and patted his silky neck. "Well done. That showed him! I was scared for a minute there."

"It was very brave of you to try to scare that creature away. Thank you, Eleanor."

"I didn't really think about it. I knew you were scared and wanted to help. I'd hate for anything to happen to you," she said fondly.

Comet nuzzled her arm and she breathed in his sweet apple-scented breath.

"Hey! What do you think you're doing, letting your dog scare my herd like that!" called an angry voice.

Eleanor looked up to see a girl coming toward them on a bay pony with a white star on its forehead. She looked about twelve years old and was frowning fiercely. Luckily, she seemed to have missed Comet's magic display.

"It wasn't my . . . ," Eleanor began.

But the girl was too angry to listen. "Not your fault, huh? Don't you know the forest code? All dogs have to be kept on leashes!"

"I know. I've seen the signs. I was trying to tell you that it wasn't my dog!" Eleanor said patiently. She mounted Comet so she could explain to the girl properly from up on her horse. "It just came out of nowhere. I don't know who it belongs to, but Comet scared it off because the ponies were about to bolt."

"Oh, I didn't realize." The girl's face cleared and she looked embarrassed. "It was good of you to get him to do that. Sorry, I tend to speak first and think later."

"That's okay. It was an easy mistake," Eleanor said generously.

"Nice of you to say so. You could easily have chewed my head off about it!"

"I'm not that hungry!" Eleanor joked.

They both laughed.

The girl introduced herself. "I'm Francine Boyd, but everyone calls me Frankie. That's a gorgeous pony you've got there. Is he forest-bred?"

"Um . . . yeah. Comet's pretty special," Eleanor said, smiling to herself. *If only Frankie knew how much!* "I'm Eleanor Gale. I'm staying at Oak Cottage with my Aunt Pippa for the summer," she said, changing

the subject quickly and hoping to avoid
any more awkward questions.

Frankie nodded. "I thought I hadn't
seen you around here before. Your aunt's
a photographer, isn't she? Dad said that
a woman who takes incredible photos
of the forest ponies had moved into the
empty cottage."

"That's right. Aunt Pippa's got an

exhibit in town next week," Eleanor said, smiling at Frankie.

Now that the misunderstanding had been cleared up, the older girl seemed really friendly. Eleanor hoped Frankie might be someone she could get to know better. It was wonderful having Comet as a friend, but it would be extra fun having a pony-crazy friend!

Frankie returned her smile. "I was just going to have my lunch. Would you like to share it with me?" she offered. "It's such a nice day that I brought a picnic with me. I often do when I'm out with Jake, checking on our ponies. There's a pretty stream near here. The ponies can have a drink while we sit and eat."

"Sounds great, thanks!" Eleanor said delightedly. "Is that okay with you?"

she whispered to Comet so that Frankie couldn't hear.

Comet nickered an agreement. "I would like to stop for a while."

As Frankie moved forward on Jake, Comet pricked his ears and followed. Eleanor reached forward to pat his silky neck.

"I'm glad we met Frankie," she whispered.

"Me too. I like her," Comet neighed enthusiastically.

Eleanor looked up in alarm to see if Frankie had heard him speak.

Comet seemed to know what she was thinking. "Do not worry, Eleanor. Only you can hear what I am saying. To anyone else it sounds like a neigh or a snort."

"Oh, okay. Good to know," Eleanor whispered back, hiding a grin.

Comet was full of surprises. She wondered what else he could do.

Sunlight slanted through the trees and made dancing yellow coins of light on the grass path as Eleanor, Comet, Frankie, and Jake rode along together. Eleanor felt a stir of happiness. There was nothing better in the whole world than to be out riding on such a glorious morning— especially on a magic pony!

Chapter
FIVE

Eleanor felt pleasantly full as she
lay on her stomach in the warm grass.
Frankie's cheese and tomato sandwiches
and chocolate brownies washed down
with apple juice had been delicious.

It was beautiful in the grove under
the spreading beech trees, with the stream
bubbling over rocks some distance away.
After a long drink of cool water, Comet

was nibbling a patch of sweet grass a few feet away. Frankie's pony, Jake, stood beneath a tree, dozing in the shade.

Eleanor had just finished telling Frankie about her aunt's three ponies. "They're called Mary, Jed, and Blue. We're going out looking for them after lunch. I hope we get to see them."

Frankie laughed. "Well, don't hold your breath! Forest ponies can wander off and be gone for weeks and then just when you think you'll never see them again, they'll start hanging around at the end of your road for ages. It's a good thing your aunt's got Comet, too, so you can ride him while you're staying with her. I'd hate it if I couldn't ride."

"Me too. It's what I love doing the most," Eleanor said. She thought it was best to let Frankie assume that Comet belonged to Aunt Pippa; otherwise she didn't know how she was going to explain him. "How many ponies do you own?"

"We've got fifty at the moment. I won't tell you all their names, you'll never remember them!" Frankie said, grinning.

"Fifty!" Eleanor echoed. "How do you keep track of them all?"

"It takes practice, but I'm used to

it. We've always had forest ponies.
Our family has been commoners
for generations. Dad's great-great-
grandmother had six mares. All our
ponies are descended from those."

"Wow! That must have been a
really long time ago." Eleanor was very
impressed. She'd love to live in the forest
and work among the ponies like Frankie
and her family. It would be her dream job
when she grew up.

Eleanor glanced at her watch.

"Oh gosh! Look at the time. I've been
gone for a long time. Aunt Pippa will be
wondering where I am. I'd better go!"

"You can blame me for making you
late by inviting you to lunch, if you'd
like!" Frankie said cheerfully. "It's the
least I could do after blaming you for that

loose dog. Why don't I ride back to Oak Cottage with you? I can explain everything to your aunt."

Eleanor was tempted. She was eager to spend more time with this friendly girl and her pony, but she could hardly ride up to her aunt's house on Comet. She imagined trying to explain to her astonished aunt how she came to be riding a fully tacked-up pony.

"Thanks, but I'll be fine," Eleanor said, hoping that with luck she and Comet might even beat Aunt Pippa back to the cottage.

"Okay then, but if your aunt gets mad at you, tell her to call me!" Frankie gave Eleanor her number. "Are you busy tomorrow? I could show you around the forest tomorrow morning if you'd like. I know all the best rides."

"I'd love that," Eleanor said, mounting Comet. "Bye for now!" she called as he broke into a trot.

"Bye!" Frankie called after them.

Comet had no trouble finding his way back. He stopped in a clump of trees just out of sight of the cottage to let Eleanor dismount. The moment her feet touched the ground, the tack disappeared in a small shower of sparks.

"It's too bad you can't make yourself invisible or something, then you wouldn't have to hide in the forest. You could stay here in the back garden, and I'd be able to sneak out and see you all the time," Eleanor suggested.

Comet blinked his intelligent violet eyes. "That is an interesting idea. I will try out these new powers. I am not yet sure about all the things I can do in this world," he mused.

Eleanor felt a surge of affection for the chestnut pony. She reached up and gave him a swift hug. "Maybe we'll find out more about your magical powers together?"

Comet twitched his ears. "Yes, Eleanor. I think we will."

Eleanor lowered her arms and stood back. "I'd better go. I'll come out to you again soon, and we can look for Destiny again," she promised.

"Very well." Comet tossed his mane and sped away.

Eleanor watched him until he was out of sight and then walked out into the open. She was opening the garden gate when her aunt came out of the kitchen.

"Oh, there you are, Eleanor. I hope you haven't been too bored," Pippa said.

Eleanor smiled. "I've been fine. I had a great time . . . um, exploring." *If my aunt only knew!*

Pippa suddenly looked at her in astonishment. "Why on earth are you wearing your riding gear?"

Eleanor could have kicked herself. She'd completely forgotten about the boots and hat! She thought quickly. "I was . . . um, in the garden when Frankie Boyd came past on Jake," she said, improvising like crazy. "We were talking about her family's ponies and stuff. She offered to let me ride one of them. So I ran inside to get my gear, while she went to get the pony. We didn't go far, just for a short ride."

Her aunt smiled. "I'm glad you met Frankie—you were safe enough in the forest with her. The Boyds are well respected around here. It sounds like you had a good time. I'm glad the two of you got along well. Especially since I ended up taking longer than I'd meant to."

Pippa shook her head slowly. "I'm starting to think that I should postpone this exhibit until after you've gone home. It's not fair for you to have to spend so much time by yourself."

"I don't mind!" Eleanor said quickly, sensing an opportunity. "Besides, I don't have to, now that I've met Frankie. We're going to hang out again tomorrow."

"It sounds like you and Frankie have things all figured out," Pippa said, smiling.

"We do!" Eleanor replied spiritedly.

Pippa put her arm around Eleanor's shoulders, and they went into the cottage together. "To be honest, I'm relieved. I was starting to worry that you'd get bored and wish you hadn't come to stay after all."

"I wouldn't think that, Aunt Pippa. I love being here with you!" Eleanor assured

her truthfully. She didn't mind at all that
her aunt was so busy. It meant she could
spend lots of time with her new, magical
friend.

"I'm very glad about that," Pippa said,
smiling fondly. She handed Eleanor a
paper bag, which Eleanor hadn't noticed
until now. "I was passing a bookstore and

thought you might like this."

Eleanor opened the bag and took out a book. *"Big Book of Horses and Ponies of the World,"* she read. "Thanks so much. I love it!"

"Time for lunch, I think," Pippa announced. "And didn't I promise that we could go out and look for Mary, Jed, and Blue this afternoon?"

Eleanor beamed at her aunt, wondering how she was going to eat a second lunch. "I can't wait!"

Chapter SIX

Eleanor spent a happy afternoon roaming in the forest with her aunt. They seemed to walk for miles. They often saw glimpses of ponies through the trees, and Pippa took a few photographs. Predictably, there was no sign of Jed, Blue, or Mary.

That evening, Aunt Pippa cooked a special dinner. Eleanor was allowed to help make an apple pie, which made her feel very grown up.

She slipped out into the garden to speak to Comet before she went to bed, but he didn't answer her call. Eleanor guessed he was deep in the forest looking for Destiny and couldn't hear her.

That night she had a vivid dream. In it she saw Destiny disguised as a forest pony, galloping along one of the winding trails. Comet's twin sister leaped across a stream and left a single glowing, violet hoofprint in the soft mud. Eleanor awoke abruptly with the strangest feeling that her dream was true. She decided she would tell Comet tomorrow morning.

The next day Eleanor got up early. After breakfast she said good-bye to her

aunt. "I'm off to meet Frankie. See you later!"

"Have a good time!" Pippa called, waving.

Eleanor walked a little into the forest and called to Comet. She planned to ride him out of sight of the cottage to meet up with Frankie where they'd parted yesterday.

Comet stepped out of the trees and snorted and tossed his mane.

"Hello, Comet!" she greeted him warmly. She noticed some small patches of dried mud on his side. Picking a large handful of sweet dried grass, she began brushing him down. "I came out to see you last night before I went to bed, but you were gone. Were you looking for Destiny?"

Comet nodded. "I searched for a long time."

"Did you find any signs of her?" Eleanor asked him.

Comet shook his head sadly. "I saw many more ponies, but Destiny was not with them. And I did not find any glowing hoofprints to show that she had passed by."

"But I think I did!" Eleanor said excitedly. "I saw Destiny in a dream. She left a glowing hoofprint in the mud near a stream. It's almost like Destiny sent me a message in my sleep!"

Comet's bright violet eyes lit up with fresh hope as he reached around to nuzzle Eleanor's arm. "Perhaps she did. It would be just like her!"

Eleanor smiled, pleased to see that he looked less sad. "We can keep a lookout for her today while we're out with Frankie and Jake." She flicked the last traces of mud away and then threw the grass down. "There, finished."

"Thank you, Eleanor."

She felt a familiar tingling down her spine as deep-violet sparkles glimmered once again in Comet's chestnut coat. When they faded, he was fully tacked up, like last time. Eleanor mounted and they set off at a canter.

They were just in time. Frankie and Jake were riding toward them through the trees.

"Hi!" The girls greeted each other, while Comet and Jake touched noses— saying hello in pony fashion.

"It looks like Comet and Jake are already friends!" Frankie said, grinning as they set off, riding abreast.

It was fun to ride into the heart of the forest with Frankie and weave through narrow, lesser-known trails without worrying about getting lost. They glimpsed a number of wild ponies, spread out among the trees. "That herd belongs to one of our neighbors, Mr. Toms," Frankie commented.

"How do you know?" Eleanor asked. She was glad for a reason to stop, so that Comet could check if Destiny was one of them.

Frankie explained that you could recognize different commoners' ponies by the way their tails were cut. "See that one?" She pointed to a gray pony that stood with its back to them. Its tail was cut into a series of blunt steps. "All of the Tomses' ponies have their tails trimmed like that."

Comet had been looking around. "Destiny is not here." He blew air out of his nostrils sadly.

Eleanor patted his neck as he rode down a track, which was bordered by hedges of hawthorn and brambles and then opened into a long, flat clearing. It was a clear run that stretched to the edge of some open fields.

"We can let the ponies have some fun," Frankie said, urging Jake on.

"Yay!" Eleanor yelled, pressing Comet into a gallop.

She could sense the magic pony's enjoyment as he went faster. He was exciting to ride, and she loved the feeling of the wind whistling past them.

"That was amazing!" she said when they had slowed their ponies to a trot.

Frankie smiled. "Wait until you see where we're going next!" She led the way to where there were some fallen logs. "I often come here to practice jumping," she said. "Jake loves it. Watch this."

She pressed her pony on so that Jake sped up and easily cleared the log. Frankie patted the bay pony's neck. "Good boy! Now you!" she urged Eleanor. "Let's see what Comet can do!"

Eleanor clicked her tongue. Comet didn't hesitate. He leaped forward. Three strides, two strides, one stride . . .

Comet soared through the air and landed safely on the other side of the log.

"Way to go! He almost looked like he was flying!" Frankie exclaimed.

Eleanor bit back a grin.

"You were fantastic!" she whispered
to him with her back to Frankie.

"I enjoyed it, too," Comet said.

The ponies took turns going over the
jumps. After a stop for lunch and a chance

for the ponies to have a drink, they went for a more leisurely ride along the grass border beside one of the public roads.

As the afternoon wore on, the girls and ponies headed back to Oak Cottage. Eleanor stopped under the cover of the trees to say good-bye to Frankie and Jake. "Thanks so much. We had a wonderful time! Can we meet up again tomorrow?"

"I don't think I can. Some of the commoners are having a roundup," Frankie explained. "It can get a bit hectic so I'll probably have to give Dad a hand. I know! Why don't you and Comet come and watch? It's pretty exciting. Visitors aren't usually allowed, but you'll be okay with me. I'll talk about it with Dad. It'll be great for you to see so many forest ponies in one place."

A New Friend

"I wouldn't miss it for anything!"
Eleanor waved as Frankie rode away.

Chapter SEVEN

That evening it poured with rain—an intense downpour that lasted for hours and cast a dark veil over the forest.

Eleanor was curled up on the squishy sofa, reading her new horse and pony book, but she couldn't concentrate because she was worrying about Comet. She knew he'd probably found shelter under the trees, like the other sturdy forest ponies, but

unlike them, he was all alone and missing
Destiny.

Her aunt was working in her office at
the front of the house, so Eleanor decided
to risk going outside to check on Comet.
Grabbing an umbrella, she hurried
through the back garden and entered the
forest clearing.

"Comet," she called softly.

There was no answer. No chestnut
pony stepped out of the trees and came
toward her. She waited a little longer, but
the magic pony still didn't appear.

"Comet? Where are you?" Eleanor
called again. She thought she heard his
voice, but it was very faint, as if it came
from far away.

"I am here . . ."

Where was he? Puzzled, Eleanor went

back into the house. She decided that
she would have to wait until morning
to go out and look for him. She was just
dumping the dripping umbrella into
the stand in the hall when she heard his
gentle whinny again.

"Eleanor. Come closer. I am here . . ."

Comet sounded a tiny bit louder than
before and seemed to be calling from
upstairs. Curious, Eleanor went up to her
bedroom.

She stood in the open doorway and
looked around. She could sense that
something was different, but what? Her
gaze fell on the table next to her bed.
There beneath the lamp stood a little
toy horse with a fluffy chestnut coat, a
pale mane and tail, and sparkling deep-
violet eyes.

As Eleanor watched, the toy horse shook itself and twitched its tail.

"Comet?" Eleanor gasped. "Is it really you? That's so cool!"

"I found another way of using my magic!" Comet told her proudly in a tiny soft neigh that matched his new size. She smiled delightedly at her amazing friend. "Now you can stay in my room whenever you want and sleep on my bed. I can even carry you in my shoulder bag and take you out with me!"

"I did not think of that. It sounds like it would be fun!" Comet said.

Eleanor picked him up very gently and sat on the patchwork quilt with him on her lap. Comet was handsome as a chestnut pony and very beautiful as his true golden-winged self—but right now he was the cutest and fluffiest miniature pony she had ever seen.

She was so engrossed in admiring Comet's tiny neat hooves and little pointed ears that she didn't notice the bedroom door swing open.

"I thought I heard you come up here. I was just going to make some hot chocolate and wondered if . . . my

goodness! What *do* you have there?"
Aunt Pippa exclaimed, her eyes widening.

Eleanor froze in shock, but it was too
late to hide Comet.

"It's . . . um . . . I was just . . . ," she
faltered. Her mind was a total blank.

"What a gorgeous little toy pony!"
Pippa's face softened as she came forward.
"It's perfect in every detail. Did Frankie
give it to you?" she asked.

Aunt Pippa thinks Comet is a toy? Huh?
Eleanor frowned in confusion. She could
feel Comet's heartbeat against her fingers
and see him twitching his ears and tail.
She couldn't believe that her aunt hadn't
noticed.

"Um . . . yeah. It's cute, isn't it?
I'm calling him Comet," she said. "It
was nice of Frankie—I really like her.

She asked me to go out again with her tomorrow. There's going to be a roundup of some of the commoners' ponies. She said that I could go and watch."

"You really are pony-crazy, aren't you?" Pippa said, looking thoughtful.

"I am! Ponies are the most wonderful things in the entire universe!" Eleanor sang out.

Her aunt laughed fondly. "I won't argue with that!"

Eleanor quickly slipped Comet behind her back and gently tucked him between her pillows, just in case her aunt felt like looking at him more closely.

"You'll enjoy the roundup," Pippa said. "The Boyd herd has the best pedigree around here. Their ponies bring in good prices. There'll be other commoners with their herds there, too. I think I'll come with you. It'll be a chance to get some good photographs."

"Sounds good," Eleanor said, so relieved by the change of subject that she wasn't really concentrating. As soon as her aunt had gone downstairs to make the hot chocolate, she turned to Comet. "Phew! I was so worried when she came in.

What just happened? I don't get it."

"I used my magic again, so that only you can see me move and hear me speak," Comet said. "Anyone else will think that I am just a fluffy toy."

"I never know what to expect with you. I love having you as a friend," Eleanor said, grinning from ear to ear. Suddenly, her face fell. "Uh-oh. Did Aunt Pippa just say that she was coming with us tomorrow to take photos of the ponies during the roundup?"

Comet nodded his tiny head. "I think that she did."

Eleanor groaned. "Oh no!"

So far she had managed to keep Aunt Pippa away from Frankie so that her aunt wouldn't find out about Comet being a life-size pony! She chewed her lip as

she wondered what might happen when
Frankie and her aunt talked, as they were
bound to do tomorrow.

What on earth was she going to do?

Chapter EIGHT

"There's nothing else to do. I'm going to have to walk over to meet Frankie and think of some excuse as to why I'm not riding you," Eleanor decided as she fastened her boots the following day. "I just hope that Frankie doesn't start asking Aunt Pippa where *her* pony Comet is. And why I'm not riding him today!"

"Thank you for helping me, Eleanor. I know it has not always been easy for you," Comet said gratefully.

"I wouldn't have it any other way," Eleanor said fondly, stroking the tiny pony's fluffy coat. "It's a shame you have to stay behind, though. There's a good chance that with so many ponies around, you'd find Destiny among them."

"I think so, too. That is why I *am* going to come with you," Comet said.

"But how? You can't do that without giving yourself away." Eleanor stopped as she realized what Comet meant. "Oh, I get it. You're going to use your magic to stay as a fluffy toy? Great idea. I'll get my shoulder bag!"

She found the bag and laid it on the floor with the top open. Comet jumped

inside, lay down, and folded his legs
beneath him.

Downstairs, Aunt Pippa was ready
to go. She was holding her camera. "All
set?" she said, smiling as Eleanor came in
with her bag over her shoulder.

Eleanor nodded.

Pippa smiled warmly. "We'll soon
be able to have lots more days out. My
exhibit's almost up and running now.

I really appreciate how you've been so
patient and understanding about having to
entertain yourself."

"That's okay. I was never bored,"
Eleanor said. There was no chance of that
with Comet around!

The forest smelled fresh and new. Large
drops were dripping from the trees after
last night's heavy rain. But the sunshine
was already drying the ground as Eleanor,
Comet, and Pippa set out to walk toward
the roundup area.

"We'll go this way. It's a shortcut,"
Aunt Pippa said, turning on to a stony
track that wound between tall field maples.

They had been walking for about ten
minutes when Pippa suddenly stopped.

"Well, look at that," she whispered,
pointing to three ponies that were nibbling

the short grass. "There's Jed, Blue, and Mary. They always turn up when you least expect it."

Eleanor watched delightedly as her aunt called to her wild ponies. Recognizing her voice, they lifted their heads, ears twitching. As they walked toward Pippa, Eleanor saw they were all wearing their fluorescent collars for night safety.

"It's best if you keep your distance. They know me, but it can be dangerous for a stranger to approach them," Pippa warned.

"They're gorgeous," Eleanor said, admiring her aunt's ponies. Mary was a dark bay with a gentle face, Jed was a lively looking gray with a black tail, and Blue was a sweet, little brown pony with black points.

Pippa took some slices of apple and

carrot out of her pocket. "I always have
some treats with me," she told Eleanor.
Her ponies munched happily for a few
moments, then, as Pippa, Eleanor, and
Comet walked on, they went back to
grazing.

"I'm glad I got to see them at last,"
Eleanor said.

She and her aunt continued down

the path, which widened and opened
into an oval-shaped clearing ringed with
flowering bushes. Eleanor opened her
shoulder bag so that Comet could look
out as they walked.

Aunt Pippa noticed Comet's tiny
legs, which were looped over the bag's
opening, and smiled. "How sweet. You've
brought Comet with you!" she observed.

Eleanor nodded, smiling. "You're . . .
er, never too old for a cuddly toy."

The sounds of voices and ponies
came toward them through the trees, and
Eleanor knew they must be getting close
to the roundup area.

Suddenly, she did a double take and
stopped dead in her tracks.

Stretching ahead of them and curving
out of sight was a faint line of softly

glowing violet hoofprints.

Eleanor heard Comet's excited voice from inside her bag. "Destiny! She has been here!"

Eleanor gasped. Did that mean that Comet was leaving to go after her? "Can you tell where she is? Is she somewhere close?" she whispered to him anxiously.

"No. The trail is cold. But it proves that Destiny came this way. When I am close to where she is, I will be able to hear her hoofbeats. And I may have to leave suddenly . . . without saying good-bye."

"Oh." Eleanor felt a sharp pang as she realized that she would never be ready to lose her magical friend. "I was hoping that once you found Destiny, you might both stay here with me," she said in a small voice.

Comet shook his head. "It is not possible. We have to return to our family on Rainbow Mist Island. I hope you understand, Eleanor?"

Eleanor nodded sadly, and her eyes pricked with tears. She swallowed hard as she decided not to think about Comet leaving and promised herself instead that she was going to enjoy every single moment spent with him.

Up ahead, Aunt Pippa had stopped to wait for her. "Is something wrong, honey?" she asked, frowning with concern at Eleanor's sad face. "No, I'm . . . er, fine," Eleanor said, making a big effort to cheer up. "I had a cramp in my side, but it's gone now."

"Good. We're almost there." Eleanor hurried to catch up with her aunt. The sounds of voices, ponies snorting, and car doors slamming were even louder. Despite her worries, Eleanor found herself looking forward to seeing Frankie and Jake again.

They emerged to one side of a group of buildings and wooden pens, some of them already filled with ponies of all ages.

Cars and trucks were parked all around and lots of people stood around in groups. Others were watching their ponies being treated by vets.

"Hi, Eleanor!"

It was Frankie. She was standing next to a large pen with a man who looked so much like her that he had to be her father.

Eleanor waved, grinning, and she and her aunt began walking toward them.

Just then, two men on horseback appeared. They were trying to get a herd of nervous ponies to go into an empty pen. There was a sudden loud bang as a car backfired. A large roan pony rolled its eyes and squealed in fright. It plunged sideways, avoiding the pen. Other ponies followed it, blindly galloping after the big roan in their terror.

The horsemen tried to get the ponies under control. But it was too late. People scattered in all directions as the ponies stampeded.

"Look out!" someone shouted.

Eleanor gasped. The ponies were thundering straight toward her and Aunt Pippa. And Comet couldn't use his magic to save them without giving himself away!

Chapter NINE

"Quick! Eleanor! Get behind a tree!"
Aunt Pippa shouted to Eleanor.

With only seconds to spare, Eleanor
leaped sideways, but her foot skidded on
a wet leaf and she went sprawling. Her
shoulder bag slipped off, and the toy pony
fell out and rolled over and over, coming
to rest under a bush.

As Eleanor struggled to her feet, she

felt the now-familiar tingling sensation
fizz in the tips of her fingers and saw the
bush sparkle with pretty violet light.

Time seemed to stand still.

Comet exploded out of the trees.

He leaped toward Eleanor, shielding her

with his body as he faced the oncoming
ponies. Rearing up onto his hind legs, he
whinnied a warning.

The ponies swerved in all directions,
pounding past Eleanor and narrowly
missing her with their flying hooves. The
second they were past, Comet glanced at
Eleanor to check that she was unhurt and
streaked away into the forest.

Aunt Pippa ran over and helped
Eleanor stand up as men on horseback
galloped past them in pursuit of the loose
ponies.

"Are you hurt?" her aunt asked,
white-faced.

"No. I'm fine. Just a bit shaken up,"
Eleanor said, catching her breath. *Thanks
to Comet*, she thought.

"That chestnut pony came out of

nowhere, but I'm very glad it did! It saved you from a nasty injury. I wonder who it belongs to," Aunt Pippa said.

Eleanor didn't answer.

Just then, Frankie ran up, too. "Eleanor! What happened? We couldn't see back there."

"The loose ponies missed me. I'm okay now. The show's over!" Eleanor joked to show that she really was fine. Hoping that everyone would stop fussing, she walked determinedly toward the pony pens. "Come on. I don't want to miss anything!" she called.

They reached the pens just as a man holding a clipboard made an announcement. The pony sale was about to begin. An air of excitement hung over the crowd as the bids started.

Frankie's dad came over to introduce himself. "You must be Eleanor. Frankie's told me about you."

Eleanor smiled at him. "Hi. Pleased to meet you, Mr. Boyd."

Mr. Boyd turned to Aunt Pippa. "I'm a great admirer of your photographs, Ms. Treacy. I look forward to seeing your exhibit."

"Thank you. Nice of you to say so," Pippa said, smiling. "I'm hoping to take a few photographs today . . . among other things," she said mysteriously, looking sideways at Eleanor.

Eleanor frowned, puzzled. What did her aunt have in mind?

But before she could find out, Eleanor heard a sound she had been hoping for and dreading at the same time.

The hollow sound of galloping hooves overhead.

She froze. Destiny! There was no mistake. And if Eleanor could hear her, then Comet must be very close.

Eleanor set off into the forest at a run. "There's something I have to do!" she called over her shoulder.

She raced through the trees. The magical hoofbeats sounded louder and very close now.

As she reached a thick clump of bushes, a twinkling rainbow mist floated down around her. She looked up to see Comet in his true form—a sturdy chestnut pony no longer. Sunlight gleamed on his noble head, magnificent golden wings, and cream coat. His flowing mane and tail sparkled like strands of spun silk.

"Comet!" Eleanor gasped. She had almost forgotten how beautiful he was as a Lightning Horse. "You're leaving right now, aren't you?" she asked, her voice breaking.

Comet's deep-violet eyes lost a little of their twinkle as he smiled sadly. "I must, if I am to catch Destiny and save her from our enemies."

A heavy wave of sadness washed over Eleanor, but she knew she was going to have to be brave. She ran forward and threw her arms around Comet's shining neck. "I'll never forget you!"

He allowed her to hug him one last time and then gently stepped backward. "Farewell, my young friend. Ride well and true," he said in a deep musical voice.

There was a final violet flash of light, and a silent fountain of rainbow sparkles fell like soft rain around Eleanor, crackling as they hit the ground. Comet spread his wings and soared upward. He faded and was gone.

Eleanor wiped her eyes. Something glittered on the ground. It was a single shimmering wing-feather. Reaching down, she picked it up.

It tingled against her palm as it faded to a cream color. Eleanor tucked the feather into her pocket. She would always keep it to remind herself of the wonderful adventure she and Comet had shared. She was so proud that the magic pony had chosen to be her friend.

When Eleanor stepped out of the trees, Frankie ran up to her. "There you are. Your aunt's looking for you!"

Eleanor looked over Frankie's shoulder to where her aunt stood holding a gorgeous chestnut pony by its head collar. The pony had a sandy mane and tail and gentle deep brown eyes. "Come and meet my new pony, Eleanor. It's time I bought one to ride, and you can

exercise her whenever you come and stay with me. I think perhaps you deserve a pony in your life aside from Comet."

"Wow!" whistled Frankie. "How lucky are you?"

Eleanor grinned as she realized Frankie didn't know that her aunt was referring to what she thought was her niece's toy pony.

"How would you like to choose her name?"

Eleanor thought of Comet on his journey to find his twin sister. She hoped they were reunited soon. "Thank you so much, Aunt Pippa. I'd like to call her Destiny."

About the
AUTHOR

Sue Bentley's books for children often
include animals, fairies, and wildlife.
She lives in Northampton, England, and
enjoys reading, going to the movies, and
watching the birds on the feeders outside
her window. She loves horses, which she
thinks are all completely magical. One of
her favorite books is *Black Beauty*, which
she must have read at least ten times. At
school she was always getting scolded for
daydreaming, but she now knows that she
was storing up ideas for when she became
a writer. Sue has met and owned many
animals, but the wild creatures in her life
hold a special place in her heart.

Don't miss

Magic Ponies: A Special Wish

Coming soon

Magic Ponies: A Twinkle of Hooves
Magic Ponies: Show-Jumping Dreams

Don't miss these
Magic Kitten books!

Don't miss these
Magic Puppy books!